MARIA-DOLORES TRUJILLO

Healing
Our Emotional
BODY

HEALING
OUR EMOTIONAL BODY

MARIA-DOLORES TRUJILLO

ACKNOWLEDGMENTS

This book would not have become a reality without the support of all my clients, who over the years gave me the opportunity to get to the root of their ailments by allowing me to read the messages from their bodies.

I want to thank God for giving me the inspiration and courage to follow my heart's desires becoming a practitioner in the healing art of Naturopathy, Aromatherapy, Nutrition, and Emotions. I am humbly aware that it is my privilege to serve as an instrument of our Creator.

I also want to acknowledge my assistant Becky Heaton for her input, talent, and support helping me to review this book, and for encouragement.

THIS BOOK IS DEDICATED TO ALL MY DEAR CLIENTS,

AND TO YOU THE READER

TABLE OF CONTENTS

INTRODUCTION

I want to congratulate you for reading this book on Healing the Emotional Body. The information contained in this book is for educational purpose only, and if you are reading this book it is because you are ready for this information.

It is presented as an alternative approach to daily health care, awareness, and prevention.

You will learn:

- How negative emotions can be the cause of body ailments.
- How the body talks, especially when it is under constant emotional pressure.
- How to use daily routines to help maintain a healthy emotional body.

Our health reflects our emotions and feelings.

Negative emotions and feelings produce powerful energy that, if not released, may concentrate on specific areas, like organs of the body. When this happens, your body's vital health is negatively impacted, affecting its natural vital health.

An emotion is any conscious experience characterized by intense mental activity and a certain degree of pleasure or displeasure. Scientific discourse, however, has drifted to include other meanings and, technically, there is no consensus on a definition.

Emotion is often intertwined with mood, temperament, personality, disposition, and motivation. According to some theories, cognition is also an important aspect of emotion.

For example, the realization of our believing that we are in a dangerous situation and the subsequent arousal of our body's nervous system (rapid heartbeat and breathing, sweating, muscle tension) is integral to the experience of feeling afraid. Other theories, however, claim that emotion is separate from and can precede cognition.

Either way, we look at it, emotions are complex. It is interesting to note that according to some theories, they are states of feeling that result in physical and psychological changes that influence our behavior. The physiology of emotion is closely linked to the arousal of the nervous system with various states and strengths of arousal relating, apparently, to specific emotions. Emotion is also linked to behavioral tendency. Extroverted people are more likely to be social and express their emotions, while introverted people are more likely to be more socially withdrawn and conceal their emotions.

Emotion is often the driving force behind motivation, positive or negative. According to other theories, emotions are not causal forces but simply syndromes of components, which might include motivation, feeling, behavior, and physiological changes, but none of these components is the emotion itself. Nor is the emotion an entity that causes these components.

Emotions involve different components, such as as subjective experience, cognitive processes, expressive behavior, psychophysiological changes, and instrumental behavior. More recently, emotion is said to consist of all these components.

Research on emotions have increased significantly over the past two decades with many fields contributing including psychology, neuroscience, endocrinology, medicine, history, sociology, and computer science. The numerous theories that attempt to explain the origin, neurobiology, experience, and function of emotions have only fostered more intense research on this topic.

"Emotions can be defined as a positive or negative experience that is associated with a particular pattern of physiological activity."

Emotions produces different physiological, behavioral and cognitive changes. The original role of emotions was to motivate adaptive behaviors that, in the past, would have contributed to the survival of humans. Emotions are responses to significant internal and external events.

WHAT ARE EMOTIONS?

AH! EMOTIONS THE STORY OF OUR LIVES

According to the encyclopedia:

Emotion is the complex psychological experience of an individual's state of mind as interacting with biochemical (internal) and environmental (external) influences.

Feelings are a response to an emotional state, detected outside and as a result of the interpretation of the body by the stimuli of what we feel through inputs. These inputs are external that we internalize and they are interpreted by the body (feeling).

Below are some examples of feelings that are expressed by our emotions:

- Taste
- Sight
- Smell
- Heat
- Cool
- Pain
- Pleasure
- Imbalance
- Pressure
- Motion

Emotions are interpretations of the feeling or feelings. Our emotions as expressions of feeling affect our behaviors, attitudes, and thoughts, which in turn affect our bodies. Emotional interpretation of a feeling varies in intensity and complexity from individual to individual.

Emotions are what the feelings mean to us, yet feelings and emotions are often used interchangeably. We can experience the feelings and the reactions in our bodies as muscular tension, pain, hot spots, head and stomach ailments, skin eruptions, and an array of symptoms. Over time, some of these temporal reactions may become chronic and quite serious.

Sometimes feelings are physiological, and sometimes they are mental. Either way, the feeling is what triggers our emotions, which can have a positive or negative effect on the body, by giving pleasure or discomfort, fear, anxiety, alarm, well-being, contentment, etc. When we become aware of our body's signals, we experience emotional sensations that can last for a short time or that can persist for a longer period. These sensations can be slight or intense.

Feelings in and of themselves are not emotional, but they trigger emotions which can cause us to want or not want, be satisfied or dissatisfied, to yearn or be content, feel well or ill. When we have what we want, then we have emotions that are satisfied; when we don't have what we want, we are unhappy. Our behaviors and emotional expressions are the results of our emotional state of want or a satisfied state.

Temperament is an expression of the personality — we are born with. Likely, our personality 'temperament' is genetically acquired and then further influenced by the type of care we received when we were young and from the world around us. Some people are born with a peaceful disposition while others have a nervous or irritable one. Temperament is the platform on which moods and emotions occur. If someone's temperament is negative it would be difficult for that person to become suddenly optimistic. The basic individual temperament can affect the emotional response to a feeling or feelings.

Moods are typically shorter-term emotional states, lasting for hours or days. However, some moods may develop into life-long behavior. A bad mood can be the result of bad weather, an occurrence at work, breaking your mobile phone, an argument with a friend, etc. Likewise, good moods can come from a compliment, a success in life, or a delicious meal. In a way, **we are the masters of our moods**. An easy temperament is more likely to glide through the various moods of life. An uneasy one may hang on to those moods for too long, making life difficult.

Emotions, often called feelings, include experiences such as love, hate, anger, trust, joy, panic, fear, and grief. Emotions are related to, but different from, mood. Emotions are specific reactions to a particular event that are usually of fairly short duration. The mood is a more general feeling, such as happiness, sadness, frustration, contentment, or anxiety that lasts for a longer time.

Although everyone experiences emotions, scientists do not all agree on what emotions are or how they should be measured or studied. Emotions are complex and have both physical and mental components. Generally, researchers agree that emotions have the following parts: subjective feelings, physiological (body) responses, and expressive behavior.

The component of emotions that scientists call subjective feelings refers to the way each individual experiences feelings, making this component the most difficult to describe or measure. Subjective feelings cannot be observed; instead, the person experiencing the emotion must describe it to others, and, to complicate the matter, each person's description and interpretation of a feeling may be slightly different. For example, two people falling in love will not experience or describe their feeling in exactly the same ways.

Physiological responses are the easiest part of emotion to measure because scientists have developed special tools to measure them. A pounding heart, sweating, blood rushing to the face, or the release of adrenaline in response to a situation that creates intense emotion can all be measured with scientific accuracy. People have very similar internal responses to the same emotion. For example, regardless of age, race, or gender, when people are under stress, their bodies release adrenaline; this hormone helps prepare the body to either run away or fight, which is called the "fight or flight" reaction. Although the psychological part of emotions may be different for each feeling, several different emotions can produce the same physical reaction.

Expressive behavior is the outward sign that an emotion is being experienced. Outward signs of emotions can include fainting, a flushed face, muscle tensing, facial expressions, tone of voice, rapid breathing, restlessness, or other body language. The outward expression of an emotion gives other people clues to what someone is experiencing and helps to regulate social interactions.

Adrenaline (a-DREN-a-lin), also called epinephrine, (ep-e-NEF-rin), is a hormone, or chemical messenger, that is released in response to fear, anger, panic, and other emotions. It readies the body to respond to threat by increasing heart rate, breathing rate, and blood flow to the arms and legs. These and other effects prepare the body to run away or fight.

"Fight or flight" is when the body 's sympathetic nervous system is activated due to the sudden release of hormones, stimulating the adrenal glands to release the adrenaline and noradrenaline, which causes several changes in the body, including an increase in heart rate and blood pressure.

WHAT IS EMOTIONAL HEALING?

We experience emotional distress in all sorts of ways: sadness, anxiety, addictions, unproductive obsessions, unwanted compulsions, repetitive self-sabotaging behaviors, physical ailments, boredom, and as variety of anger, bleak, and agitated moods. What helps relieve this distress? What helps a person to heal? What is emotional healing?

When life takes a toll on the body, many of us may develop emotional states that are debilitating or that somehow negatively affects our overall lives. For some, it can be situational, like moods. But, for others, it can be manifested into lifelong conditions, which can include both; physical and mental illnesses.

Emotional healing begins by taking responsibility for our actions, emotions, life history and physical state of being.

We cannot say that others "made" us do or feel or act on something. Sometimes our emotions are unwell because we are unwell. Although other people or influences may be instrumental, the responsibility for emotional well-being is ours to make.

By identifying our emotions and becoming aware of the messages the body gives us, we begin the healing process.

During this process, ACCEPTANCE and APPRECIATION are very important: Acceptance of where we are at that moment; and appreciation for the awareness and opportunity to heal.

When we desire to heal, we desire to turn things around for the best. It could be to heal the body of an illness, to heal a relationship, or to mend a financial situation; whatever it is, we long for the same results: HEALTH, BALANCE, and HAPPINESS.

One of the first tasks at hand in a successful healing journey is working at reestablishing the greatest possible measure of **inner peace and confidence**.

No matter how long it takes, we have the resolution to learn from our mistakes; and to work along the process using the appropriate tools, **like forgiveness. A tool that provides the break of chains of dysfunctional behavior from the past made physical in the present.**

There are many paths to this end including prayer, inner silence, contemplation, religion, exercise, healthy diet, and/or a relationship with a pet. It is learning to re-channel the thinking that could, otherwise, lead to disquiet and distress, or even illness.

Emotional healing allows us to come to terms with events and circumstances which have occurred in our lives. Once emotional healing work is done to release past emotional blockages, we not only integrate these experiences into our lives, **but we** allow ourselves to grow and develop emotionally; on a deeper, more profound level.

Emotional healing involves integration of the fragmented parts of our deeper self by not only understanding a past experience, but to also resolve it fully, so that it no longer evokes an emotional response whatsoever. With emotional healing, the past traumatic experience will no longer control our thoughts, feelings and emotions. Instead, limiting belief systems will be overcome and lasting, positive change will take place on a deeper level.

There are many programs, courses and books available that can help an individual overcome specific problems, like anger management, increased self-esteem, improved confidence, weight loss, and substance abuse. While most of these problems can be overcome using specific techniques, it is when we go deeper into the problem to look at the cause and release its emotional impact that real change occurs. Change that is transformative in nature; will release the emotional charge behind the emotional block or pattern.

We start creating change by getting our first tool, a JOURNAL, which more than **a tool, is a companion during our healing journey!**

Writing in our JOURNAL as a daily practice will help us to keep center and focus on our inner selves. Begin by writing when waking up or before going to sleep.

EXERCISE:

In your journal answer these questions:

What do I need to accept?

What do I need to be grateful for?

Who do I need to forgive?

When starting to experience an emotion, stop, and ask "Where in my body do I feel it and, how does it make me feel?"

AFFIRMATION

I accept Harmony and Balance by doing one task at a time. By taking one step at a time, and by doing one thing every day out of pure love.

I accept and appreciate the beautiful energy of love in my life and my state of consciousness.

NEGATIVE VS. POSITIVE EMOTIONS

Emotion is an expression of energy. An emotion comes from within as an interpretation of an event. The body responds energetically to the feeling it interprets with emotions. The expression of the emotion results in a physical response: how we feel, our behavior, thoughts, and all this affects our bodies.

The body is like a giant circuit board and a memory storehouse. Every cell in our body responds to every thought we think, every word we say, and every image we see.

Emotions are mental results of feelings and are associated with particular organs and functions of the body. When blocked, they will vibrate to a corresponding organ or system of the body. For instance, anxiety is felt immediately by the stomach and intestines. If we carry fear, worry or anger in our minds, and keep those emotions bottled up inside without release, they are capable of triggering changes in the body. These changes, while imperceptible at first, eventually manifest in imbalances.

Negative emotions and negative thinking create heavy and dense vibrations, able to slow down the vibration of life. These slowed vibrations are fundamentally at odds with the natural rhythms we are born with. When they are expressed, they can produce body behavior that can change the vibration of our bodies. Holding on to these vibrations will upset the chemical balance in the body, giving away our power and creating illness.

Positive emotions and positive thinking, on the other hand, create light feelings that produce a normal and healthy balance. They encourage a flow that must be kept moving through the mind for wellness to be maintained.

Healing starts by becoming aware of our thoughts and how they can be changed. This, in turn, will help us to take control of our belief system. Negative emotions can keep us in limited and negative states;

when we release them and redirect them to positive feelings, healing takes place with a lasting transformation to our physical and emotional bodies.

Emotions can keep us hanging on to our fears and we can get stuck having difficulty moving forward. We may develop an attitude of solitude, not engaging ourselves in enjoyable activities, or not participating in certain events due to our fears. These fears can manifest as issues such as claustrophobia, or other phobias that keep us stuck.

Thus, fear contributes to a tendency to escape and anger to a tendency to attack. Negative emotions seem to narrow our action repertoires (or actual behaviors). When running from danger we are unlikely to appreciate a beautiful sunset.

This function of negative emotions can help minimize distractions in an acute situation. Positive emotions, on the other hand, are not associated with specific actions. So what good are they, apart from the fact that they merely feel good? What is the point in feeling happy or joyful, affectionate or ecstatic?

When we experience positive emotions our thinking and attention lean towards our creative side and we are more open to express joy, contentment, and to see opportunities instead of obstacles. We become more open-minded and flexible.

Experiencing a positive and negative emotion at the same time seems to be difficult since one can negate the other, but we can experience a state of joy than can be altered rapidly by very sad or shocking news.

Our health can be impacted positively or negatively. If we experience joy, happiness, contentment, affection, or love, our body becomes resilient and will have the ability to cope with the everyday stresses of life. But, if we experience anger, resentment, frustration, hate, guilt, or grief, our body can have difficulty coping with events and eventually manifest it as a physical illness.

Emotions associated with love, enjoyment, or satisfaction will give us a playful disposition to build our social skills and positive interactions with others, such as enjoying time with friends.

As a result, experiencing positive emotions will elevate our mood, self-esteem, desire to use our creativity and our God-given talents. They build a positive character and help our bodies to stay healthy and in balance.

Experiencing negative emotions, in contrast, decreases our body's capacity for healing, and the ability to bounce back quickly after an unpleasant event.

EXERCISE:

In your Journal, describe:

What positive emotions did I feel today?

What negative emotions were bothering me today?

AFFIRMATION

I choose to love myself by setting boundaries, listening to my inner guidance, and trusting my heart.

I am delighted to express joy, enthusiasm, and contentment.

EMOTIONS AND SPIRITUALITY

Our emotions can affect us spiritually. **The energy or life force flowing through our bodies** is the source of our enthusiasm, vitality and inner well-being. When this life force is not expressed and gets disrupted or stuck, the person's zest for life is diminished, leading them to have difficulty coping with life so that facing challenges and responsibilities becomes a difficult task to perform.

Emotional tension constricts life's energy as much as a muscle contract after injury. It could inhibit circulation, cause fatigue, affect focus and concentration, and eventually can affect the person from being fully responsive and in the moment. Emotional pain from past childhood trauma can manifest in the physical or psychological in adulthood. Emotions are the body's natural responses to life experiences, being a communication system expressing the person's inner reality from moment to moment.

Forgiveness is a virtue. We can use it as a tool to heal and break the chains of the past. It makes space for Love to come in and Anger or Fear to move out.

Learning forgiveness can provide a way to release traumas from a dysfunctional family behavior. This forgiveness can help individuals repair relationships with parents and grandparents or anybody else involved. In doing so, one allows the life force to flow naturally and easily through the body. This life force not only impacts the emotional brain, but it also maintains the immune system and improves the body's capacity for healing itself.

Spiritual healing represents growth. It requires listening to the messages the body gives. Without it, the body becomes numb or shut off. When the body is shut off due to emotional numbness, this creates dependency on others and addictions. Spiritual healing requires taking care of ourselves, taking responsibility, having trust, and faith. Altogether, this will enable us to be independent to fully experience our life and spirituality.

By taking these steps we can restore our body, mind, and our health, allowing ourselves to grasp how everything in life is interconnected.

Emotions provide a much better gateway to the spiritual dimension of our lives than beliefs. Awe and wonder are emotions particularly associated with spiritual experiences. Calm, joy, and contentment are among other emotions that typify mature spirituality.

The spiritual dimension looms largest in extreme situations, like when someone is faced with great challenges or a major loss. Unsurprisingly, the path to positive feelings often lies through more adverse emotions, such as foreboding, or even terror. Stark bewilderment, rage, deep shame, self-blame, and intense sorrow may also be provoked.

This, of course, is all part of the natural order of human life. The wise approach is to trust the process of emotional healing and growth toward maturity.

Ultimately, adjusting to one's fate and acceptance of loss brings the necessary results. This release of emotions is uncomfortable, such as when sadness is accompanied by tears. People often resist crying, and apologize for it. But in reality, it is an essential part of the healing process.

When the storm of grief does eventually pass, however long it takes, serenity is restored and a new level of happiness, contentment, and equanimity arises. When it does, and often unexpectedly, after a period of considerable struggle, feelings of humility, gratitude, and wonder are experienced. Renewed clarity, as bewilderment and confusion subside, revealing a new level of spiritual understanding of wisdom. Recognition that everyone else faces similar troubles in their lives increases compassion and loving-kindness towards others.

Why, then, is everyone not already emotionally and spiritually mature? One reason concerns the very strong emotional likes (attachments) and dislikes (aversions) that naturally come into play. Each of us have emotions we seek to avoid and those we prefer. For example, the natural tendency is for people to prefer joy over sorrow and calm over anxiety, but, of course, the reality of this is not so simple when you consider our patterns or habits of emotional experience and expression.

Feeling bad about feeling bad is one example of this kind of problem. Some people are deeply averse to anger. It scares them. When a situation arises to provoke anger, anxiety rapidly takes over instead. This short-circuits the natural process of energy flow through the full spectrum of emotions. If anger is not expressed this will provoke resistance, therefore, such people are at a disadvantage. Even worse, their anxiety and inability to fight back against loss and injustice can give rise to a handicapping degree of inadequacy. It also predisposes them to being exploited by those who seem to be emotionally stronger.

Feeling good about bad feelings is the reverse of the same problem. So, on the other hand, rather than being averse to anger, some people are attached to it. Anger is a strong feeling and it gives them a sense of power and often a dominating behavior of control, whether accurate or not, of being in the right. This predilection for anger often overrides doubt.

Some people, consciously or otherwise, seek opportunities to get angry, searching for faults in others, for example, or by engaging regularly in arguments and other forms of winner/loser behavior (usually biased in their favor). An attachment to anger thus covers up a wish to avoid shame as well as doubt. It protects against other emotions, like anxiety and sadness, too - but at a price. When a person's emotional life defaults towards anger, this has destructive consequences for the person concerned. Both the range and spontaneity of their emotions are limited.

There are consequences where others are concerned too. People may feel unduly coerced or bullied, and seek to avoid those who seem unreasonable – and ultimately selfishly – angry much of the time.

When any of the other emotions are similarly strongly either preferred or avoided, there are negative repercussions. Excessive shame (in today's terminology, 'low self-esteem') is a painful problem for many. An excessive sense of self-worth, on the other hand, soon leads to quick-tempered vanity.

What can be done? How can we learn to accept our emotions as they arise, change in nature and intensity, and eventually fade? How can we learn to be less attached to some and averse to others? Problem recognition is the first step: knowing that something needs to be remedied. This means paying close attention to our own emotional profile. Which emotions do we prefer, and which do we try to avoid? This question, in itself, is beneficial. Seeking help, finding an effective remedy and making a commitment to change come next. Using that remedy on a regular, disciplined basis will lead towards progress and maturity. This is certain, just as wound healing is certain if the wound is kept clean, free of infection, and dressed regularly. Nature takes care of it.

What are the remedies? Seeking help is always a good place to start. For myself, I find that when I use simple techniques and I maintain commitment and discipline daily, I am able to keep my own emotions in balance, responding to the pressures and stress of life with grace and flexibility.

Taking the Next Step:

MY REMEDIES FOR A GRACEFUL LIVING

1. Five virtues:

    Forgiveness and Tolerance are the remedies I use to address anger.

    Contentment gives me comfort and peace; the remedy I use for greed.

    Discrimination or good judgment I use to choose what is good for my growth or what is a waste of time.

    Humility, my remedy when I face vanity.

    Detachment the remedy for attachment. When I practice detachment, it helps me not to get involved in the drama of a situation.

2. My special time with God or the Holy Spirit:

    A daily practice, which I do at the same time for 15 or 20 minutes. I like to start by closing my eyes, and quieting my mind, then, I place my attention on the area between my eyebrows and sing: May the Blessings Be! Or the word HU, a love song to God.

    During this contemplation, I see myself in a safe, calm and beautiful place, and then I listen to the Holy Spirit. I surrender to the Divine. I listen and listen.

It takes daily practice and love in my heart to approach the altar of God, but doing it with consistency the rewards I receive are an expansion on my awareness, help to experience Deep Love, and control over my own negative emotions.

When I come back from my contemplation, I write in my journal what I received, what I saw, and what I heard.

Usually, the best creative ideas, the best answers on how to resolve a problem or a situation, the best ways to addressing a program for a client, or even the creation of all my formulas have come to me through my time with God.

3. Gratitude

    An invaluable Remedy! Abundance flourishes through a grateful heart. Abundance is not only about money but about quality of life. When we are grateful for everything we receive our health, relationships, work, finances, etc., keeps abundance flowing.

4. Putting Love in everything we do.

    Love is the catalyst to manifest our thoughts and desires into reality, then, and, by our free will, we take action and magic happens. Love is a very powerful emotion. Its vibration can change our perspective of life. When we put love in everything we do, we go the extra mile, and this has the unique quality of accomplishing a job well done.

5. Surrender

    We do our best. We do the best we can and the best we know. And then, we release it to God or the Holy Spirit. When I surrender my cares, fears, and negative emotions to the Divine, this gives me peace, and a sense of support, and protection.

EXERCISE

Daily, in your Journal, write 10 things you are grateful for.

I am grateful for:

AFFIRMATION

I open the door to the Holy Spirit, letting the Light and Sound come through to change my life according to HIS will.

HEALTH: BALANCING OUR FOUR QUADRANTS

The four quadrants of our life are **PHYSICAL, MENTAL, EMOTIONAL** and **SPIRITUAL.** They are all connected. If one is out of balance, the rest will be affected.

PHYSICAL

Our physical health is the result of our understanding that eating well, exercising, giving the body rest, relaxation, and enjoyment are the key elements to maintain a healthy and fit body.

It is our lifestyle choices that can affect the most precious possession we have: **OUR HEALTH.** If we lose it, we lose the ability to accomplish our tasks and responsibilities. Our quality of life diminishes, becoming poor and bored and, feeling like life is passing by us and we are not part of it. This can set us into depression, lack of enthusiasm, apathy, fear, or worry.

Any life crisis will place demands on our nervous and immune systems. If we maintain a healthy body and mind, we will be able to face with ease, poise, and grace the unexpected events that life may throw to us, so that our health does not fall apart.

MENTAL

The mind perceives and understands objects; it is the perception of the outer world that a person will respond with a calm, and relaxed attitude or agitated, anxious behavior.

The state of our mind reflects the state of our physical, emotional and spiritual well-being. If a person has a calm attitude and a stable mind, this influences his or her behavior in relation to others. In other words, if someone remains in a state of mind that is calm, tranquil and peaceful, external surroundings or conditions can cause them only a limited disturbance. But it is extremely difficult for someone whose mental state is restless to be calm or joyful even when they are surrounded by the best facilities and the best of friends.

This indicates that our mental attitude is a critical factor in determining our experience of joy and happiness, and thus also our good health; our state of mind plays a crucial role in our experience of happiness and suffering.

Learning effective mental health principles can be very effective in overcoming issues related to stress, anxiety, and depression. Clear focus, correcting negative thought patterns, eliminating self-limiting beliefs, learning how to manage anxiety and stress, and overcoming obstacles are keys to a healthy life.

EMOTIONAL

It is said that emotions operate on many levels, having a physical and psychological aspect. They bridge thoughts, feelings, and actions, affecting many aspects of a person. And, simultaneously, the person affects many aspects of the emotions.

When emotions are not expressed and/or released but buried within the body, they may be a cause for a serious illness. The chemical reactions that anxiety, fear, frustration, negativity, and depression can cause are very different from those caused by happiness, contentment, love, or acceptance.

- The two basic emotions are: Love and Fear
- Change is constant in our lives producing situations that may result in one or the other
- Situations that are the result of fear may produced anxiety, anger, sadness, depression, inadequacy, confusion, hurt, loneliness, guilt, and control, or shame are fear-based.
- Situations that are the result of love may produce joy, happiness, caring, trust, compassion, truth, contentment, satisfaction are love-based.

Fear can not stand the healing energy of Love

Fear-based emotions stimulate the release of one set of chemicals while love-based emotions release a different set of chemicals. If the fear-based emotions are long-term or chronic they may damage the systems of the body. When our systems weaken, many serious illnesses may set in. This relationship between emotions, thinking, and the body is being called Mind/Body Medicine today.

SPIRITUAL

We may think that we are limited to just our physical body and state of affairs, including gender, race, family, job, and status in life. But, we are more than that. We are Souls and we exist because God loves us.

When we allow ourselves to be filled with inspiration, which also translates into love, joy, wisdom, peacefulness, and service, we create harmony or a sense of inner peace.

"Letting go and letting God" is a way to get out of the way and allow our Creator or a higher power to do what is best for us. It is also an act of surrender that will help us release the restrictions that we put on ourselves.

In my spiritual journey, I have learned that **happiness is a state of consciousness and attitude is everything.** When I still my mind and make my inner connection with Divine Spirit, the knowledge I receive helps me to understand that living a spiritual life means living gracefully, smoothly and effectively.

When we are disconnected from Divine Spirit, we become vulnerable and it is easier, then, to open the door to the influence of negative emotions.

EXERCISE:

In your journal, make a list of what your physical body is telling you based on your thoughts, your emotions and your connection with Divine Spirit for each one of the four quadrants.

PHYSICAL   **MENTAL**

EMOTIONAL   **SPIRITUAL**

HOW TO IDENTIFY OUR EMOTIONS

Our emotions are an indicator of what is going on inside of us. Identifying how we feel about a person, place, situation or event will give us information about our personality and perceptions.

Some people prefer to work with their emotions in silence, while others do it with friends, a family member, or a therapist. Other people prefer to write about their emotions and still, others will use a more casual approach.

When emotions are blocked they will vibrate to its corresponding organ. This, in turn, inhibits the body's capacity for healing itself. This stuck energy is the source of many ailments. Our defense mechanisms work very effectively to hide emotions from consciousness, and it is often a challenge to what one feels.

We often don't have any idea how we feel. We seldom take our emotional temperature and assume that what we feel is what we're consciously aware of. What we know superficially is all there is:

I'm in a good/bad mood today; work's stressing me; I'm not angry, I just don't feel like talking; I don't feel anything.

We're satisfied with that answer and accept it as something we just have to live with.

But we don't have to just live with it. There are tools that we can learn to help us identify what feelings are cooking beneath the surface that have more to do with our current state of affairs than we'd imagine.

Perhaps the answer to "I don't even know how I feel" is becoming aware of our behavior in daily life. How is my home life? Am I getting along with my partner? My children? My parents and siblings? How am I doing at work? Am I enjoying my work? Am I getting along with my co-workers? My boss?

We can take our emotional temperature by describing: What feelings am I aware of having? Which is the most prominent? When I became aware of this feeling? These questions may lead to others and likely take us to different places perhaps not traveled before. We may be surprised at details or memories that haven't been available to us before.

Identify the stressors: What might be triggering this feeling? What's happening (or not happening) in our daily lives? It helps to deconstruct one's day, week, month. Paying particular attention to events (thoughts, dreams, etc) that we have no control of and perhaps have decided 'not to pay attention to' because we cannot change them. This is a common pitfall. The fact that we have no control itself brings an emotional reaction.

This is particularly important when it comes to the threat of illness—if we receive the news of having an unidentified mass on an organ, it could be ours or of a loved one, we can't help but get frightened, anxious or even depressed, as we assume the worst. The reality is that life events are always about change, and this generates feelings getting us out of our comfort zone.

The fact is, the more we admit our fears to ourselves and to our loved ones, the more likely they are to diminish in size. When feelings are denied or dismissed, they do not diminish in size or disappear. They intensify. If we think of knee pain, for example, the more and longer we neglect it, the louder and more insistent it gets.

THREE ELEMENTS OF EMOTIONS

THE SOURCE: Feelings are senses to our external and internal response inputs.

THE RESPONSE: Emotions are the complex responses to those feelings.

THE LOCATION: Emotions may be felt in our bodies in various ways, such as muscular tension, pain, hot spots, or inflammation.

WHEN WE ARE STUCK ON OUR MOODS AND BEHAVIORS WE MAY EXPERIENCE EMOTIONS OF:

- WANTING
- NOT WANTING
- HAVING
- NOT HAVING
- SEPARATION

EMOTIONS OF **WANTING** MAY BE EXPRESSED AS:

ANTICIPATION, GREED, HOPE, ENVY, DESIRE

EMOTIONS OF **NOT WANTING** MAY EXPRESSED AS:

FEAR, SHAME, REPULSION, ANXIETY, APATHY

EMOTIONS OF **HAVING** MAY BE EXPRESSED AS:

HAPPINESS, PRIDE, GUILT, GREEDY, DOMINATING, DEMAND-ING, JEALOUSY

EMOTIONS OF **NOT HAVING** MAY BE EXPRESSED AS:

ANGER, SADNESS, DISTRESS, INADEQUACY, JEALOUSY, RE-SENTMENT

EMOTIONS OF **SEPARATION** MAY BE EXPRESSED AS:

ATTACHMENT, GRIEF, UNLOVED, REJECTION, VULNERABLE

OTHER EMOTIONS THAT MAY BE EXPRESSED ARE:

SURPRISE, AMAZEMENT, ASTONISHMENT

MESSAGES FROM THE BODY

Messages from the body:

The body is always speaking to us. If we pay attention, we can understand what each message is trying to convey.

We already said that there are two basic emotions: Fear and Love

Fear may manifest as anxiety, anger, hesitation, insecurity, nervousness, scared, defensive, worry, self-doubt, tension, vulnerable, or wanting to scape.

Love may manifest as patience, understanding, caring, contented, flexible, agreeable,

INTERNALIZED EMOTIONS OPERATE INVISIBLY FOR A TIME, THEN MAY BECOME PHYSICAL AND MAY ADVERSELY AFFECT A CORRESPONDING ORGAN

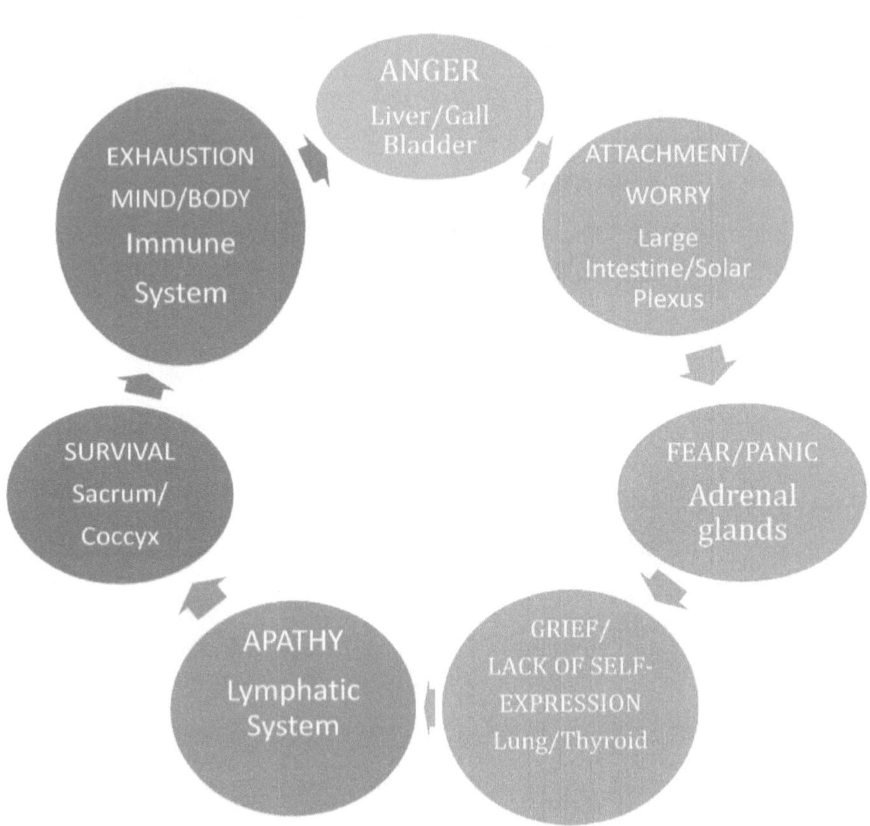

WHEN NEGATIVE EMOTIONS DISRUPT THE BODY'S ENERGY THE RESULT MAY BE EXPERIENCE AS:

FEARS ANXIETY PANIC	ANGER GRIEF PHOBIAS	DEPRESSION TRAUMATIC MEMORIES

WORRY GUILT LIMITATIONS	ATTACHMENT APATHY SURVIVAL

Lavanda Aromatherapy Botanical Products can assist with the healing of the physical and emotional body:

Fears, Anxiety, Panic: Emotional Support
Confidence Blend
Calm-Relax

Anger, Grief, Phobias: Liver Support
Heart Support
Fearless

Depression, Traumatic Memories: Emotional Support
Lip and Eye Formula

Worry, Guilt, Limitations: Lymphatic Support
Calm-Relax
Detox

Attachment, Apathy, Survival: Fearless
Lymphatic Support
Lung Support

Heart Support

These products are available at www.ailavanda.com

EXPRESSIONS THAT REFER TO DIFFERENT EMOTIONS AND THE ORGANS THAT MAY BE AFFECTED

When experiencing two or more of these expressions, ANGER could be present and may affect the Liver.

I WON'T….
YOU CAN'T MAKE ME …..
I HATE THAT
I WILL GET EVEN
THAT IRRITATES ME

When experiencing two or more of these expressions, ATTACHMENT and/or WORRY could be present and may affect the LARGE INTESTINE and/or the SOLAR PLEXUS.

I CAN'T LET GO
I MUST BE IN CONTROL
I HAVE GOT TO LET GO
I FEEL OUT OF CONTROL
I FEEL ANXIOUS
I WORRY ABOUT EVERYTHING

When experiencing two or more of these expressions, FEAR OR PANIC could be present and may affect the ADRENAL GLANDS.

WHAT IF IT DOESN'T WORK?
I GOT TO HAVE IT
WHAT IS GOING TO HAPPEN TO ME?
I AM ALWAYS TIRED OR FATIGUED
I AM FEARFUL ABOUT…..

When experiencing two or more of these expressions, GRIEF could be present and may affect the LUNGS and/or the THYROID.

NO ONE UNDERSTANDS…
THERE IS NOTHING I CAN DO
I AM VERY SAD….
IT HAS ALWAYS BEEN MISSING
IT IS DIFFICULT TO ENDURE
I AM GRIEVING OVER….

When experiencing two or more of these expressions, APATHY could be present and may affect the LYMPHATIC SYSTEM.

I AM NOT GOOD ENOUGH
I DO NOT FEEL LIKE IT
I CAN'T DO IT
WHAT IS THE USE?
I DO NOT KNOW HOW TO SAY IT
I DO NOT KNOW HOW TO DO IT

When experiencing two or more of these expressions, PAIN (physical or emotional) could be present and may affect the SACRUM, and/ or COCCYX areas. Difficulty in being grounded or lack of libido may also be present.

WHY THIS HAS BEEN DONE TO ME?
IT HURT TOO MUCH
I CAN'T BEAR IT ANY MORE
THE MISERY SEEMS ENDLESS
I DON'T HAVE THE SUPPORT I NEED

When experiencing two or more of these expressions, DEEP EXHAUSTION could be present and may affect the MIND and BODY. A lack of ENERGY and CONCENTRATION could also be present.

I AM EXHAUSTED
I DO NOT FEEL ANYTHING
I AM NOT AWARE
AM I GOING TO MAKE IT?

RELEASING EMOTION

When we experience a situation that we find difficult or painful, and we are not able to cope with the pain, or we are just afraid of it, we often get busy doing something else so that we avoid facing it. If we repress our emotions, the energy of the feelings become real and may get stuck in our muscles, ligaments, stomach, and other areas of our bodies.

There are many different actions we can take to deal with our emotional pain. Most of the time our behavior is to ignore and in turn help us escape reality.

We may pretend that the situation has not happened, or eat comforting foods loaded with sugar and fat, we may indulge in excessive eating, drinking, or recreational drugs; using prescription drugs such as tranquilizers, to induce relaxation.

A very common behavior is excessive reading, shopping, watching TV, or working (to becoming workaholics) with no time for family or enjoyment. Behaviors like these manifest as a way out for not feeling the pain, facing the problem and giving a solution.

TO HELP OURSELVES TO OVERCOME THIS BEHAVIOR, WE HAVE TOOLS AVAILABLE TO USE DAILY SO THAT OUR LIVES WILL GO SO MUCH SMOOTHER. THE TOOLS HELP US TO BECOME AWARE OF OURSELVES, AND WHAT TAKES PLACE AROUND US.

ALSO, THEY WILL HELP US TO STAY AWAY FROM THE EVERY DAY DRAMA OF LIFE, THEREFORE, WE DO NOT DWELL IN THE CLASSIC VICTIM CONSCIOUSNESS.

**TRANSFORMING STUMBLINGS BLOCKS
INTO HEALING STEPPING STONES
USING OUR TOOL KIT**

1. PROCRASTINATION:

Nowadays, life goes very fast. We live in a constant state of rush, from the moment we get up until it is time to go to bed at night. In this fast-paced environment, we become accustomed to thinking in a particular pattern, so much so that we do not realize or become conscious of our desires and dreams, and if we do, we tend to procrastinate in not taking action exploring **Our Desires and Goals**.

We forget to listen to our heart, to pay attention to its whispers of what we desire about having, being, accomplishing, etc.

The JOURNAL is a wonderful and very valuable tool. In previous chapters, I mentioned using a JOURNAL for the exercises. If you have one and have been doing the exercises, CONGRATULATIONS!

If you do not have one yet, get a JOURNAL and use it every day as a practice of centering and focusing on oneself. Start writing first thing when waking up or before going to bed.

Our first tool is a JOURNAL!!

The key to overcoming procrastination is taking action daily and doing one thing at a time.

EXERCISE:

In the Journal write:

How do I feel today?

Example: I feel insecure, fearful, angry, etc.

What is my goal today?

Example: To take responsibility and look into the situation that keeps me locked. I do my part by taking action to neutralize the negative into positive.

What do I desire to accomplish today?

Example: I desire to feel confident, courageous, satisfied and feel joy today!

With this exercise, we focus on:

The feeling, the goal, and the desire.

We can combine the tools in our tool kit with the remedies given previously.

For instance, if I feel angry, fearful and insecure, the remedies can be the virtues of Forgiveness/Detachment/Contentment.

First, I take responsibility:

<u>For my feelings</u>

Nobody made me feel this way. It is my choice to go through this experience as a victim or as a winner learning my lesson and transforming it into a success.

I am the captain of my ship. I use my God-given talent of Creativity to master my experiences in the Sea of Life as stepping stones on my Journey to Self-Mastery.

Second, I take action:

Action means I take responsibility and I do one thing at a time, step by step without overwhelming myself.

AFFIRMATION

I forgive myself for experiencing anger, fear, and lack of confidence.

I choose to detach myself from the situation that caused these feelings and by the virtue of Contentment, I transform them into Courage, Confidence, Trust, and Satisfaction.

This can be written in the journal, and also saying it out loud and with <u>a real desire</u> for transformation.

2. ATTACHMENTS TO THE PAST

<u>We say they are non-important but it still hurts</u>

Sometimes we try to hide what affect us and make ourselves believe that it is not important when the reality is that it hurts. When we keep remembering every little detail about a particular event or situation and go over and over on our heads, it can become an obsession and can affect our bodies.

Our second tool RELEASE AND LET GO!!

EXERCISE:

In the JOURNAL, write about an event, or situation that caused pain. By writing about it, will help us to release it and let it go, which is a good step toward emotional healing.

We can combine this tool with the remedy of **Surrender**.

We write about it, release it and let it go, then, we surrender it to the Holy Spirit, accepting that healing will take place for our good and the good of all concern.

We do not give it another thought and go about our day doing the best we can, putting love in everything we do, which is another remedy that will help us to take action for a change.

3. LACK OF WILL AND ENTHUSIASM

<u>What makes us feel strong?</u>

There is nothing that can make us feel stronger as when we feel successful. When we place our attention on our daily successes, it is easier to eliminate fear and anger.

Putting things in writing will help us to deal with our daily challenges in a healthy way. What we did not accomplish today, will be an action to take tomorrow and again for the next day.

Patience, consistency, and perseverance are very healthy habits to acquire in the road of emotional healing. Concentrate on your Successor Successes.

Our third tool SUCCESS!!!!

EXERCISE:

Write in your JOURNAL

 Which success or successes I had today?

 What was accomplished today?

What action or actions did I take today toward accomplishing my goal or goals?

4. INADEQUACY

<u>I am not good enough, I am not worthy enough……</u>

When experiencing feelings of inadequacy and/or lack of self-confidence, FEAR is at the door disguised as self-doubt, and dread, leading us into self-sabotage. Fear can paralyze us and hold us back from taking the next step, whatever that next step may be, such as the positive desire of adopting a healthy lifestyle, pursuing a passion, or ending a toxic relationship.

Fear comes from the mind, and the mind does not like change, it is too cozy in its comfort zone, sending messages of excuses, disinterest, or doubts.

To face fear, we connect with the whispers of our heart, this is the voice of our intuition speaking through it. To listen to our heart, we find a quiet place and at a time when we will not be disturbed to go within. We let the HEART speak, not allowing the mind to interfere. Listen and Trust.

 A very special time is early in the morning, when we are still in a state of relaxation, and before we are fully awake. If we are still, keep quiet and pay close attention, we can receive important messages and information.

Our fourth tool LISTENING TO OUR HEART!!!

EXERCISE:

Close your eyes, take two or three deep breath, and say out loud or to yourself, the following:

I quite my mind.......

I invite my heart to speak.......

I am listening.........

At the end of the exercise, write in the journal the message or messages you received.

AFFIRMATION

I am so grateful for listening to the whispers of my HEART

5. I HIDE SO I DO NOT FACE THE WORLD

Finding Help:

Expressing ourselves is another way of LETTING GO and RELEASING. We might want to find help by consulting a professional counselor, therapist or a minister, who can listen and help us to understand what we are experiencing.

A close loving friend can also be a great help, specifically someone we trust, who offers us comfort and love, who does not try to resolve our issues or give us advice, but who instead listens with the heart and is there for us.

Our fifth tool EXPRESSING OURSELVES!!

EXERCISE:

Concentrate on the importance of asking the right question to obtain the answer that will help us in the right direction.

Also, concentrate on the importance of being persistent and if we get back an answer of "it is not possible" then, we keep trying in different ways or with a different approach.

Next step: Action

a) We come with a plan and create a map, showing the starting point, middle, and the accomplished end. Sometimes there are stages in between, it could be a rest point or a re-direction of the heart desire.

b) We create an image of it and visualize it, placing our attention on the area between our eyebrows.

c) We give the feeling to it: Love, Success, Satisfaction, Confidence

d) We keep quiet about it since it is still forming.

e) We release it to Divine Spirit and surrender it, knowing that the BEST will take place, for our good and all concern.

AFFIRMATION

My good is on ITS way!

6. BLAMING OTHERS

We are responsible for our actions and emotions:

Taking responsibility for our actions and emotions will help us to care for ourselves. This healthy action will get us out of the everyday drama of the mind, instead of blaming others and being in the victim consciousness.

But taking care of ourselves isn't just a healthy diet and lifestyle. It also means to know how to set boundaries for ourselves and to learn when to say no, especially if our plate is full or we simply do not feel comfortable with a particular situation that we have been asked to do.

Demanding responsibilities, high-stress levels, multitasking, or accepting something by obligation can cause emotions such as anger, giving us feelings of resentment, creating an acid pH in the body that will, in turn, develop in negative chemical reactions affecting our cells and tissues, which eventually may manifest in physical illness.

Our Sixth tool WE SET BOUNDARIES AND LEARN TO SAY NO!!

EXERCISE:

AFFIRMATION

*I use my creative God-given talent of being responsible for myself when setting boundaries.
I say No gracefully, and respectfully when facing demands
I did not ask for.*

7. CONCENTRATING ON LACK

<u>Peace and Contentment</u>

We all have, at one point or another, the tendency to look at what we do not have, what we lack, or what is missing, and this may produce anxiety, dissatisfaction, or frustration. We are so used to concentrating on what we lack that we forget to look at the blessings we already have.

Concentrating only on lack robs our peace and contentment. We keep living in the past or future. We compare ourselves to others by judging or criticizing us.

Peace and Contentment allow us to live in the present, to be satisfied with ourselves for our accomplishments, no matter how big or small they are, to be grateful for the blessings we have.

To manifest Peace and Contentment in our lives, we count our BLESSINGS and do it with GRACE AND SERENITY. These are beautiful, healthy energies, and when we express them, just like the energy of Angels, we face any challenges in life, where serenity takes us trough the flow of the event or situation with peace, and grace-giving us the contentment to see the blessings of the experience as a gift.

Our Seventh tool, GRATITUDE AND COUNTING OUR BLESSINGS!!

AFFIRMATION

I live in the now, I am grateful for all my blessings.
I practice the blessing of GRACE, the blessing of SERENITY and PEACE is with
me.

EXERCISE:

In your JOURNAL write what you are grateful for and do it with LOVE AND GRATITUDE. These positive emotions will help us to be in the frequencies of ABUNDANCE AND PROSPERITY.

CONCLUSION

Thank you for reading Healing Our Emotional Body.

I hope this information was of value to you, and that I was able to provide you with remedies, tools, exercises, and affirmations to start practicing and help you gain awareness of your emotions and their effects on the physical body.

To manifest transformation, we do it by practice, practice, practice.

If you enjoyed this book, please take the time to share your thoughts and post a review. It would be greatly appreciated!

Your review and feedback will help me to continuously improve the content in my books and make every one more relevant and helpful to you and others.

ABOUT THE AUTHOR

Maria-Dolores Trujillo is a Board Certified and registered Traditional Naturopath, Certified Aromatherapist specialized in Clinical Aromatherapy, a Certified Natural Health Professional, Certified Nutritional Consultant, Licensed Esthetician, and Educator. She is also the founder of Aromatherapy Institute, Inc., *Lavanda*® Aromatherapy Botanical Products, and Lavanda Academy, Inc.

Maria-Dolores established her aromatherapy practice while living in England. Upon returning to the United States in 1991, she introduced Clinical Aromatherapy in the Dallas, Texas area, providing consultations, skin and body treatments to her clients, and developing formulas for their home care programs. Following her highly successful practice, she created *Lavanda*®, a line of Aromatherapy Botanical Products developed from custom-made formulas.

As the founder of Aromatherapy Institute, Inc. and in Dallas, a recognized center for training and education in the field of clinical aromatherapy, Maria-Dolores created, developed and teaches all the courses the Institute offers and has gained national recognition as a leading educator in her field.

Maria-Dolores was an instructor with The National Association of Certified Natural Health Professionals teaching the courses she developed on Clinical Aromatherapy and Reflexology, in both English and Spanish, to health practitioners throughout the Country.

Through her Lavanda Academy, she created and taught various workshops such as "The Secret the Skin Reveals", "The Messages Pain Convey", "Balancing the Four" among others.

She was an Honored Professional of the National Directory of WHO's WHO in Executive & Professionals (1996-1997 edition) and was featured in Dallas Women's Magazine (1993).